That
Old River

MARY DUNCAN

To order additional copies of this book, contact:
Xlibris
844-714-8691
www.Xlibris.com
Orders@Xlibris.com

ISBN: Softcover   978-1-6698-1587-7
         Hardcover   978-1-6698-1588-4
         EBook   978-1-6698-1586-0

Print information available on the last page

Rev. date: 03/14/2022

That Old River

This is dedicated to all souls who have gone from our lives:

My native sister Tanya, who lost her high
school sweetheart and husband

My grandfather and grandmother, who
showed me the way to adulthood

Mother Bonnie, whose soul was taken
from a drug-induced woman

To all young souls who we held in arms and passed

To all souls who battled cancer and sickness

To our Vietnam veteran Mike, who
was a true friend in our lives

Buddy the Basset	Maggie
Bobby Maggee	Gypsy
Father Severes's Two Collies	Bud Royal Moon
Pudger	Caliber
Jackson	Apache
Hallie Dog	Pacthes

Remembering souls that leave us behind to only have memories of those who were lost. They may be two-legged or four-legged that came into our lives and left us with their gifts of love and true dedication to us.

I went to the Old River, down a long lonely trail, and weaved my way through the dense forest. My clothes were tattered, and my bare feet were dirty and bleeding from the thorns and stones along the path. Finally, I came to the edge of the Old River.

The river was crystal clean; snow melting high in the mountains made the Old River very cold. Rocks turn into stones from the Old River pushing them along with whitecap water rushing down the mountain. A mist hovered over the river, teardrops from a thousand angles.

As I peered into the waters, I could see my reflection. A sad face, a soul ripped apart, a heart so broken it will never be pieced back together. Tears began to drop one by one into the river, small ripples with each tear drop.

All of a sudden, the river reared up and splashed the tears from my cheeks. Then, the Old River spoke to me.

"My child, why do your tears fall into my waters? My child, why are you so sad?"

7

I said, "O Old River, my heart is broken, my soul is lost. I lost my best friend and soulmate today. I have a hole in my soul now. I lost a section of my life that will never return.

The river replied to me, "I see, my child, your pain is great, your sorrow is deep, and your soul is lost. I cannot take away grieving, but you can come to the banks anytime you wish. I will wash each tear from your cheeks and carry each one to the sea. My child, it will be okay. My mist is a tear from a thousand angels, the mist will carry sadness to the heavens."

Printed in the United States
by Baker & Taylor Publisher Services